Morgan the Motorhome Mouse and the Andersons:

Stonehenge Underground

Cate Read Hickman

Read Books

Cover illustration and design by Hannah Kilpatrick

Developmental and copy editing: Janis Hunt Johnson / Ask Janis Editorial / www.askjanis.com

Reader reviews provided by Yvonne Aileen, and by Ali Shaw, Indigo: Editing, Design, and More, www.indigoediting.com

Photographs by Marlene Schotte, used with permission, 2022

Pentangle image by Owlcation, http://owlcation/humanities/Symbolism-of-the-Pentangle-in-Sir-Gawain-and-the-Green-Knight, 2023

Celtic high cross image with decorative knot work "may be freely reused":

web.archive.org/web/20041208074429/http://www.sodipodi.com/indx.php3?section=clipart, 2023

ISBN: 9798857226445 (paperback)

ISBN-13: 979-8857226445 (ebook)

Printed in the United States of America

For my uncle, Keith Read, who wrote the Prologue and shared his original ideas for a Morgan story with me. He encouraged me for years while I was writing it—before and after my father, his brother, passed away. Thank you so much, Uncle Keith.

For my parents, Barbara and Lee Read, and for my supportive family: my amazing husband and sons.

For Ellen Wellborn, talented artist, good friend and neighbor, who passed away in Spring of 2014. Gone but never forgotten, for her gentle prodding, kindness, and inspiration. "Get busy!" she'd say.

And for Yvonne Aileen, Londa Corcoran, and Melanie—thank you.

Contents

Prologue

by Keith Read

One moonless night, a fast-moving, bus-sized object streaks through the sky, and crashes into a wooded plot on the Anderson farm. The farm is located in a small coastal town in western Oregon.

Initially, no one witnesses this phenomenon, except for a remote listening post operated by a secret organization that routinely searches for alien encounters and other suspicious events. The detection of this particular event will lead to a future investigation by this secret agency, but maybe that's another story for another time.

Shortly after sunrise, Brian Anderson is reviewing the farmhouse remote cams for any nighttime activity, when he spots the crash. Gathering his wife, Fiona, and their children, twins Aidan and Katie and their younger son,

Jeremy, they set off in their pickup, armed with a shotgun and shovel to check out what the heck happened.

At the woods, the family follow a short path of destruction to what appears to be the wreckage of an airplane-bodied craft, only slightly dented and charred. But what, or who, is inside? And are they, or is it, still alive?

Entering through a hole in the side of the strange vehicle, Dad investigates for possible bodies. Finding none, he moves cautiously forward towards the cockpit. He spots no one until reaching the pilot's seat. There, he comes across the limp form of a creature dressed in a U.S. Forest Service uniform, complete with old-style military campaign hat.

Who, or what, could this be? For this creature appears not to be human, but more resembles a mouse! A big one, between mouse and cat sized--whiskers and all! What's more, the animal is still alive, and looks pleadingly at him.

Surprised by all of this, Dad realizes that he must help. So he gently lifts and carries the "mouse" out to where he left Katie and Aidan.

Due to his prior military experience, it is at this point that Dad realizes that no one outside their family must know of any part of this incident—any governmental or other agency involved would totally destroy or discredit any truth to the matter. And would probably destroy the mouse.

As time goes by, the mouse—whom the Andersons have named Morgan—is nursed back to health by the family. He refuses any attempts to explain who he really is, or where he came from. Is he an extraterrestrial? A time traveler? From another dimension?

What is known is that he is very smart, very polite, and very mechanically inclined. Morgan and Dad (who is also very mechanically inclined) set out to repair Morgan's vessel, which Dad moved from the woods to his barn so as to eliminate any unwanted prying or curiosity from others.

When some months have passed, Morgan's ship has been transformed into what, at first look, appears to be a large, sleek, first-class motorhome. *But what a motorhome!* All the technology of Morgan's original transport has been salvaged and refurbished.

A motorhome that can *fly*? A motorhome that can travel at supersonic speed? A motorhome that can be secured for defense against any armed intruder? *Yes* to all of the above.

And so we begin the adventures of *Morgan the Motorhome Mouse and the Andersons: Stonehenge Underground.*

Chapter One

Motorhome at Night

Crack, snap, crunch. Katie woke up and sat bolt upright. Carefully moving the curtain next to her bunk in the motorhome, she peeked outside. She heard twigs crack on the ground outside their motorhome's window.

Four men stood about twenty feet away, between the family's motorhome and their house. One of the men had a flashlight and was moving it around, as if looking for something—or someone.

Katie held her breath. *Who are they? What are they looking for? Have we done something wrong? Do they know we're in the motorhome? Should I wake Mom and Dad?*

Her twin brother, Aidan, was still sound asleep in the next bunk, but Jeremy, her seven-year old brother, woke up and started dancing around with Morgan, their smiley magical mouse friend, who was somewhat larger than regular mouse size, a bit rotund, and very nimble. Morgan had joined their family years ago when he knew that they needed him. Turns out, he needed them too. Sensing the situation—something he was amazingly good at—Morgan quietly hopped onto Katie's shoulder and looked outside with her.

"Watch *Sesame Street*!" said Jeremy, who hadn't learned how to ask questions in the usual way yet.

"Shhhh, Jeremy!" Katie whispered. "Go back to sleep!" She said it just loud enough for him to hear. He had super-sensitive hearing so she knew just how loud she needed to be with him, which was barely perceptible to others without Autism Spectrum Disorder (ASD).

"Watch *Elmo*! Watch *Sesame Street*!" Jeremy insisted loudly.

Oh great, Katie thought to herself, wondering if and how she could get him to be quiet again, as he seemed totally oblivious to the situation. She figured she'd tell him exactly what was going on and ask him again to be quiet. Sometimes that worked.

"Jeremy," she whispered again, "you need to be quiet because there are some men outside and I don't want them to hear us. I don't know what they're doing."

Jeremy didn't look at her but quieted down. He seemed focused on Morgan.

"Thanks, Jeremy," said Katie, "Sleepy time now, okay?"

"Plaaaaaaay!" insisted Jeremy, loudly again.

"Play after sleep, okay?" Katie said reassuringly, hoping he'd go for it.

"Okay, sister," Jeremy agreed. He talked and sang to himself quietly, self soothing.

Relieved, Katie looked out the window again.

"Hey Boris, let's get out of here, I hear kids in there," Katie heard one of the men say.

"I figured the family was in their house, not in this here motorhome," another replied, "Yeah, let's go!"

Katie breathed a sigh of relief. "Thank goodness," she said under her breath.

"What are you doing?" asked Aidan, sitting up.

"Shhhh! Mom, Dad, wake up!" Katie whisper-shouted to her sleeping parents from across the aisle.

Their mom roused first, groggy.

"What's going on, Katie?" she asked.

"Mom, four men were outside a few minutes ago. One of them had a flashlight and was shining it all around, looking for something, I guess. They must have heard us or saw me watching them because they left. I'm scared they'll come back.

"I'll call the police. Then let's all try to go back to sleep," said their dad.

"Good idea, and no worries Katie," said Mom.

Morgan liked phones and dialed for their mom with his right paw. Not your average mouse, he had a way with numbers and electronics of all kinds, and he had memorized all the important safety numbers. He wore a special tan-colored hat with *U.S. Forest Service* embroidered in tiny green letters, probably from one of his previous adventures. It matched his cute little vest perfectly.

Aidan, Katie's twin brother, fell back to sleep fast, still full of cake from their tenth birthday party that morning, just a week before Christmas in their usually peaceful small town of Manzanita, Oregon, where they ran a several-acre Christmas tree farm on their property. They'd done well with tree sales this year, and decided to close early for the season so they could use the school holiday break to go on an important family trip.

"Sunny days, sweeping the clouds away," sang Jeremy quietly, over and over until he was asleep again, which took nearly two hours.

They always slept in their amazing flying motorhome which they affectionally named *Kubla*, the night before leaving on a family vacation so they could be ready to leave first thing the next morning.

Five hours later, the sound of the Anderson family's motorhome's engine starting up broke the quiet of the morning air. Katie woke up, startled by the sound. She smelled hot chocolate.

Chapter Two

Time to Go!

Aidan jumped on his sister's bunk.

"It's time to go!" he said. "Go get your cocoa and breakfast now or you'll have to skip them."

"What a minute," said Katie, "Did Mom and Dad find out who those men were last night?"

"Ask them later. We're out of here!" said Aidan.

Kubla had a mind of its own, but with a little help from Morgan, magic was in the air!

Mom and Dad were at the helm, while Kubla warmed up, preparing for take-off. Morgan jumped off Jeremy's bunk, spun around three times, put his left foot in and then out again, and finished off his dance by shaking his tail all about. It was their usual good-luck ritual before taking off on a family outing.

"Buckle up!" they all shouted together, as usual.

Less than a minute later, Kubla was airborne, and so were they!

Scenery was passing by quickly: lots of farmland in the middle part of the United States, then lots of skyscrapers as they passed over the east coast. Their parents stayed in the drivers' seats the whole time, and Jeremy jumped and twirled while Aidan tried to get him to sit back down and put his seat belt back on while they flew over the Atlantic Ocean.

Their mom called back to them, "We'll take a snack break soon. No worries, Morgan knows the way!"

Katie took out her tablet and with her stylus wrote:

Note to self:

1. OMG, wake up Mom and Dad sooner next time if something like that ever happens again.

2. Always eat breakfast!

They were headed northeast, flying fast. After what felt like only about two hours (but was probably a little longer), they started descending. The sky was gray and overcast, but that didn't deter Morgan. He started his landing dance to ensure their safety. This time he put his right foot out and then in, shook his tail all about, took off his park ranger cap and bowed deeply to a round of applause from the family before returning it to his head.

Landing safely on terra firma, they couldn't believe their eyes! Large, oblong, gray stones surrounded them, most standing upright, a few lying on the ground. Some of the upright ones had long stones, which Mom told them were called lintels, resting across the top of them with another stone next to it. They were all arranged in a circle, with another circle inside, made of smaller stones.

"What is this place?" Aidan and Katie asked their parents in unison.

"This, kids, is what's known as Stonehenge," their mom answered. Katie and Aidan exchanged looks—they remembered now that they had learned about it in school the previous year. Jeremy started saying, "Stonehenge" over and over.

"Jeremy, try taking some deep breaths like this," Mom said, as she modeled it for him, calming him temporarily.

"We're in England. Wiltshire, England," to be exact. I first learned about it when I was just a few years older than all of you," said their mom.

Katie grabbed her tablet, googled "Wiltshire, England," and started taking notes about it. She knew later she'd be glad she did.

Most of Wiltshire is rural and the land is made of chalk. Chalk is a type of limestone rock that is porous and resists erosion. It forms when there's a chemical reaction called precipitation, and minerals come out of water that contains dissolved calcium.

"Maybe that's why Stonehenge was built here," their mom said, answering Katie as she read aloud what she was typing. Katie continued writing her notes:

Wiltshire sits on a high downland. A downland is often called a "down," which comes from the Celtic word for "hills." It's a place with lots of open areas on top of hills made of chalk. Wiltshire's Down is famous because Stonehenge and Avebury stone circles are here. These stone circles are Neolithic monuments because they date back to 2600 BC, towards the end of the Stone Age, when people used stones to make things like tools, art, and weapons, before figuring out how to make metal. BC stands for "before Christ." Since Stonehenge was built during prehistoric times, which means before people started to record history, we can only guess as to its purpose. It might have had a religious or spiritual meaning, and likely had to do with telling time to help people figure out when to plant crops in spring or summer, or when to prepare for winter, since the whole monument is oriented towards the sunrise on the summer solstice and to the sunset of the winter solstice. It also could have been a burial ground, since a lot of very old human bones have been found here. The name "Stonehenge" likely comes from "henge" which is an old English word for "hanging" or "suspended"—suspended stones stacked horizontally on vertically placed stones, that is.

"Yes. I remember learning a lot about that when I was a kid too," their mom said. "We're here for Jeremy because Stonehenge is reputed to have healing powers.

"I like this place," Aidan told Katie as she put her tablet away in her backpack. The kids and Morgan waited outside while their mom and dad parked Kubla alongside a gigantic field of red poppies.

Even though Kubla was a magical motorhome, thanks to Morgan, it still needed some human guidance—specifically drivers—just to make sure it stayed on track.

"Arms higher!" exclaimed Aidan as he, Jeremy, and Morgan danced a highland reel.

Katie looked on, happy to see her brothers and their magical mouse buddy in such good spirits. Their mom and dad joined them.

Katie agreed, "I like it here, too!"

A low rumbling sound broke the quiet of the afternoon. They all stopped to listen. The ground started to shake. So did the stones.

Chapter Three

Secrets in Stone

They held onto each other as the shaking continued, making sure they were far enough away from the massive stones.

Crash! Boom! The thunderous sounds continued until the ground opened up about twenty yards away from them, revealing a stairway leading down into the earth. The shaking stopped. The stones were still standing.

They looked at one other and considered their options—the pros and cons of staying above ground versus walking down the mossy stone stairs. Morgan knew the answer and nodded downward to them all.

"What do you think, Mom?" asked Aidan. Usually when the family separated, Mom would stay with Jeremy, due to his medical and sensory challenges, and so accompanying behavior issues. This time, Mom and Dad exchanged a look and seemed to make a decision.

"We'll all go," said Dad. They agreed that if Jeremy had troubles due to the medical challenges of autism while there, then they would all leave quickly. Morgan's reassuring nod toward the stairs helped. He always helped guide them on these trips and had never steered them wrong. Mom and Dad trusted him. They were here to help Jeremy feel better.

"Let's all go!" said their parents together. They slowly walked down the enchanted staircase to what appeared to be a corridor, lit by torches, as if they were expected.

"Jeremy, please be quiet and try not to make any sounds until we know if it's safe to talk or not, okay?" their dad said.

"Be quiet, it's quiet time! Quiet, quiet, quiet, quiet time!" Jeremy sung to his dad, without looking at him. Dad nodded, knowing Jeremy saw him even though he wasn't looking at him.

"Mom and Dad, we're older now, so if we get separated for awhile, we'll be okay," Katie told their parents, adding, "plus, there's Morgan to protect us, remember?"

"That's true, Katie," answered their dad. "Morgan has always come through for us and kept the kids safe, even in the worst of situations," he said, looking at his wife.

Their mom answered, "Right, but let's check it out first."

At the end of the short corridor, they found two stone doors with big hinges. On the door to their left were some words carved in ancient rune. Luckily, Katie's tablet contained a language translator. She took a picture of it, then jotted down the translated words in her tablet:

NO FEAR,

ONLY LOVE.

Morgan twitched his tail twice.

Jeremy looked up at his sister. "Secret," he whispered.

Mom and Dad looked at each other. "I didn't know he even knew that word," their dad whispered to his wife.

Katie told them all what the words translated to in English.

"Well, that's a good sign," said their mom.

The door to the right had a pentangle in the middle, eye level to Aidan and Katie, symbolizing truth, honor, and goodness.

Each door also had a Celtic cross at the tip that looked like this:

Small glints of green light appeared under each door.

"How about if we just knock on each door and see who answers?" asked Katie.

"It's worth a try," answered their mom.

"Remember what Goethe said," added their dad. "Live each day as if your life had just begun."

"True for a single adult, but when it comes to keeping kids safe, that's another story," said their mom.

"Yes," agreed their dad. "But for now, let's check this out, and let's be sure to leave the doors open so we can meet back up with each other anytime we're ready. Aidan, take your brother and sister with you, and don't forget Morgan."

Mom nodded.

"Yes, I saw him twitch his tail too. Thanks, Dad," said Aidan. They had figured out Morgan's communication style over the years.

Mom and Dad drew Jeremy, Aidan, and Katie in for a big family hug, with Morgan too, of course, who was sitting on Katie's shoulder again.

Jeremy, Katie, Aidan, and Morgan chose the door on the right with the pentangle on it.

Mom and Dad faced the door to the left and knocked on it together. It opened immediately and they went inside.

Jeremy started to panic, making a few loud sounds, and Morgan consoled him right away, squeaking a familiar pattern that Jeremy recognized. Soothing patterns like counting to ten over and over again, or singing familiar songs he liked usually calmed Jeremy.

"Thanks, Morgan, said Katie, relieved, knowing Morgan had averted a meltdown that they couldn't afford in this situation.

The heavy door began to close softly behind their mom and dad.

"Wait," said Mom, without knowing yet to whom she was speaking. "We want the doors left open, please." The door stopped instantly and re-opened so they could all still reach each other if needed. That was a good sign.

"Hello," said a kind voice about five feet in front of them. Mom and Dad looked down and saw a small lavender-colored female human-like being enrobed in white and glowing. She had an ethereal quality to her that made them feel comfortable right away.

"I'm Caragh. Your beloved children and their mouse friend are about to embark on a journey—a journey different from yours here, but no less significant."

She continued, "What you must do is hold only good thoughts in your hearts and minds about them always. Don't let negativity or fear take over. Always focus on good, happiness, and health."

Their mom stopped, aware of a tinkling sound coming from the limestone rocks around them.

Back in the corridor, Katie and Aidan knocked in unison on the door with the pentangle on it, while Jeremy and Morgan stood nearby.

"There's no answer," said Aidan nervously. "Let's go catch up with Mom and Dad," he added loudly.

Jeremy picked up on Aidan's agitation and started running around them in circles. Katie was afraid Aidan was inadvertently beginning to trigger another potential meltdown for their little brother.

"Shhhh," Katie told Aidan, "no way are we leaving. Look at Jeremy," Katie warned further.

"But we don't know who and what is on the other side of the door. This is crazy!" insisted Aidan.

Jeremy started making anxious high-pitched sounds and Katie shot Aidan a look.

Morgan came to the rescue again—humming and dancing with Jeremy, who smiled and calmed down right away. Then Morgan winked at Aidan, calming him down immediately, too.

"Thanks, Morgan," Aidan said, as he regained his composure.

Suddenly, the door opened widely. They all walked through it and into what appeared to be a fog bank.

"Oh no!" Katie shrieked as the floor below them gave way to a shiny steep slide, just like the one they'd slid down in the Hallstatt Salt Mines on their Austrian adventure with Morgan last year.

They all screamed except for Morgan, who squealed with joy, as down they went.

Chapter Four

Limestone in the Down

"Courage!" Aidan yelled to his siblings, rallying again.

They landed on a floor of soft moss in a large, dimly lit cavern with high rocky ceilings. As they looked around the room, they found it was more of a valley—an underground valley—with damp limestone walls.

Katie realized that they were right below the plain where Stonehenge was built, the Down that she had made note of earlier.

No wonder it's so mossy in here with all this water on the walls, Katie thought to herself, while noticing a group of people up ahead.

"Hey, there are those four men I saw outside back home in the middle of the night before we left. Remember

Aidan?" Katie asked. "Oh wait, you were asleep. Jeremy, do you remember? They must have taken some incredibly fast aircraft to get here before we did!"

Jeremy said, "Lions, and tigers and bears, oh my!"

His siblings figured that meant he didn't remember, but it was hard to tell. Sometimes he was obviously tuned in. Other times not so much. They'd learned over the years that the autism symptoms were a result of a problem with his gut that very much affected his brain. Doctors said it came from toxin exposure, which, had they known about it, could have been prevented.

Their whole family wished that they had a crystal ball so they could know how to return him to normal. They wanted so badly to give him relief, since he sometimes hit his head hard with his little fist or with his iPad. They wanted him to have a normal life. When he'd hit himself, after they'd get him to stop they would ask him why. He told them that he was trying to fix his brain. It was heartbreaking. Sometimes he screamed loudly and threw things. They figured that was when he was in pain or overwhelmed, or maybe both.

Whatever it was, it was too hard on him and the whole family. Underneath the autism illness, they could tell he was smart, with the same feelings as everyone else. For him, it was a debilitating illness. ASD can be viewed as a strength, especially if it's mild and there is some extra-special sensitivity for perceiving enjoyable things, like colors and art. Like many things in life, it's very individual. Jeremy's kind of ASD was not that kind though, as he wasn't born with it, and it wasn't mild. His family was very worried about him and his future.

"I wonder what they're doing here," said Katie just loud enough for her siblings to hear, feeling unsure of what to do next, and trying to remain calm. She sat down on the floor.

"Since they're here, and we're here, I'll bet it has something to do with us," said Aidan.

"Katie, wake up. Are you okay?" Aidan continued.

But Katie didn't answer. Her eyes were still open as she sat there quietly.

"Sister, sister, sister!" said Jeremy, concerned.

Even Morgan tried to get her attention by doing the hokey pokey.

She stayed quiet, breathing slowly.

"How do we call 911 from down here? I want Mom and Dad!" cried Aidan. He'd already had enough and they had only just arrived in this cavernous world.

Katie started rocking, like Jeremy did sometimes to self-soothe, but instead of forward and back, she swayed from side to side.

"No fear, only love. No fear, only love," Katie kept chanting quietly to herself, continuing to sway.

"Katie, what are you doing? Are you okay? Snap out of it!" her twin said, desperate to pull her out of it and get her back to normal. He wasn't going to lose another sibling to some disorder, toxic injury, illness, disability, trauma, accident, or anything else, darn it!

"Katie, if you like, you can close your eyes and still see me," her invisible-to-others translucent self said to her, sitting about a foot in front of her. "Your brothers can't hear me. Reassure them and then join me. We have a lot to talk about."

Katie closed her eyes and nodded, and quietly told her brothers to relax and that she'd be back soon. Then she rejoined her other self.

"Did I summon you?" she asked her other self in her mind.

"In a sense," her other self answered, continuing their non-verbal conversation, "I'm always here. Sometimes you know you need me, other times you don't know but still might need me. I can help. You're never alone, even if you feel like you are. I'm you, but without the fear or other emotions."

"I must have frozen when I saw the four men with the flashlight, after being separated from my parents and not knowing what to expect. We want so much to find a cure for Jeremy, and are always having to fight off mean stuff from other people who don't understand what it's like for him, or for the rest of us, as his family. It's too much.

"Why are some people so mean?" Katie asked.

"I wish I knew," Katie's other self answered. "Maybe they're unhappy and don't understand what it's like to walk a mile in someone else's shoes. Maybe they don't know that autism is often a medical and developmental disorder, or that it can be a mild neurobiological disorder for the rare person who is born with it and then it turns out to make a positive difference for them and makes the world a better place, adding neurodiversity. They may also not know that it can be a more severe illness for those who unexpectedly acquire it after birth, through some damaging force like environmental toxins, which affects how they develop, as well as every other part of their lives. Such a small percentage of this group recovers through biomedical intervention, including changes in diet, but some do.

"It's toxins plus genetics, and for this second autism type, it could have been prevented if medical professionals and parents had known what to avoid ahead of time. More is known now, but information reaches people all too slowly. You can be like Joan of Arc, and help spread the word, and hopefully that will lead to a cure. The sooner the better.

"When it comes to mean people who don't know about autism and its various forms, and don't understand why many kids and adults with it behave the way they do, the thing to do is to leave their meanness where it originates—with them—and focus on yourself and the kind, good people in your life. They are the ones who truly care about you and want you all to be happy, healthy, and successful.

"It's good that some of the doctors you've seen for Jeremy can tell that he wasn't born with it, and can provide magnesium, vitamins, herbs, antibiotics, probiotics, and other supplements and medicines when needed to ease his discomfort.

"Remember, he is just as worthwhile as anyone else with autism, born with it or acquired, as well as anyone who doesn't have it, of course. As with cancer, it's not the person's fault that they have it. Anyone who loves him, like you, wishes he were totally well so he can have a happy, healthy life.

"Everyone deserves to be respected, healthy, and successful, and to have hope in life. Just avoid extreme doctors, as your mom said, even if they have a good reputation for helping kids with autism. She learned that the hard way."

"Should I stand up to the meanies?" asked Katie.

"Only if it would make you feel better and doesn't waste your energy," answered the other Katie, "but don't expect it to change them. *You* can be happy either way. I know it hurts that he's sick and that you all worry about his future safety and well being. You know your parents are working on it, keeping track of the latest information and waiting for a real medical breakthrough that works for everyone affected by it, not just for a few here and there. Try to keep the faith and be happy.

"Maybe mean people aren't as lucky and don't have that solid footing that you and your family do—Jeremy included," she added.

"Thank you very much. What about those four men over there? What are they up to?" Katie asked.

"Don't be afraid of those four men. You are the bravest of the brave. Look at all you've done already. They can't hurt you or your loved ones. You have a strong and loving heart. Your parents, siblings, and friends love you. You are a lot like Joan of Arc. Just keep going and doing what you know is right." The other Katie waved at her as she faded away.

Katie opened her eyes. "Okay, thanks again," she said quietly. Then she was back. "Hi, everyone!"

"Geez, Katie, way to scare us all to death!" Aidan said. "Seriously, thanks for telling us you were okay—but what the heck was that? What were you going on about, all spaced out?"

Jeremy smiled up at his sister. "Katie trance, Katie trance, Katie trance!" he said.

"Jeremy, you knew?" asked Katie, thinking back on a theory she'd read earlier about Stonehenge. She recorded it in her tablet:

Ancient people may have used the sound reverberations inside the circle to induce a trance-like state.

Maybe it somehow applied to being underground at Stonehenge, too. Whatever it was, she felt a lot better, and told her siblings about her experience.

"Sister okay," Jeremy said, hopping up and down.

"Yes I am, thanks, Jeremy. Do you have to find a restroom?" she asked him, looking around for a restroom in the large underground cavern. If that was the case, she knew they didn't have much time to find one, given the gastrointestinal issues that often accompany autism. Unfortunately, due to gut lining damage from the toxins which cause the disease for some kids, including her little brother, "gastrointestinal autistic entercolitis" was something they had to deal with.

While her brothers negotiated bathroom duty, Katie searched on "Joan of Arc," with whom she could often relate during their family quests because she wanted so much to help Jeremy recover:

Joan of Arc, or Jeanne d'Arc (in French), was a peasant girl living in medieval France. She believed that God had chosen her to lead France to victory in its long-running war with England. With no military training, Joan convinced the embattled crown prince Charles of Valois to allow her to lead a French army to the besieged city of Orléans, where it achieved a momentous victory over the English and their French allies, the Burgundians. After seeing the prince crowned King Charles VII, Joan was captured by Anglo-Burgundian forces, tried for witchcraft and heresy and burned at the stake in 1431 at the age of 19. By the time she was officially canonized (sainted) in 1920 as the Maid of Orléans, as she was known, she had long been considered one of history's greatest saints, and an enduring symbol of French unity and nationalism.

Emboldened by this passage about Joan of Arc, Katie started to put her fears aside and decided to focus on love and learning. If Joan of Arc could help the people of France back then, Katie decided that she could help *her* people: her family.

"Just keep going," Katie reminded herself. "Never give up."

Chapter Five

Where Are Mom and Dad?

"I've been expecting a visit from your family," said Caragh, who hovered before them.

"Oh?" Mom asked.

"Yes. Morgan explained everything." The tinkling sound resumed from the direction of the limestone wall. "And that just means more magic is afoot!" Caragh said giggling. "Come with me, I have something to show you."

Caragh led them through another limestone tunnel and to a small table in a well-lit room.

"You know the four men in your yard last night who were looking for something? Well, this is a map to what they were looking for, and what they still hope to find."

Dad asked, "You mean like a treasure map?"

"Exactly," Caragh said happily, her glow getting a little brighter. "I think you'll be quite pleased with what you find. It's something Morgan told me you've been seeking for some time from the medical community. It's what doctors and researchers, as well as non-traditional healers, aren't usually able to provide for families in your situation as yet, try as they might."

"We're all ears!" Mom said.

"There is a golden bejeweled amulet buried in the front yard of your home, between your house and where you usually park Kubla, out front. It's in a small bronze box, and it is hundreds of years old," whispered Caragh. "It has the power to heal your son, Jeremy, completely."

"Let's go get the kids, head home, and dig up the front yard right away!" Mom exclaimed, excited.

"Just a moment. You have competition, as you can probably imagine, given the power of such a treasure," warned Caragh. "The amulet heals only one wearer every 100 years—if it is found that is, unless there are mitigating forces."

"Thank you so much Caragh. May we take this map with us?" Dad asked.

"Absolutely! And to help guide you now and always, remember the words of Dr. Martin Luther King:

'Darkness cannot drive out darkness, only light can. Hate cannot drive out hate, only love can.'"

"Yes. This is a dream come true!" said Mom, heading for the door.

Chapter Six

The Four Men

"It's time I talk to those guys," Katie told her brothers.

"Risky," said Aidan. "Let's go. Better safe than sorry."

"It'll be okay, Aidan. Jeremy, if it turns out those men are not okay, start getting loud and wild, okay? That'll scare them off."

"Octopus! Octopus! Octopus!" Jeremy started screaming over and over.

That got the men's attention.

Shhhh, not yet!" Katie said to her brother.

For some reason, Jeremy wasn't able to stop himself, and kept going, saying it over and over for another minute or so.

"Hey over there," shouted one of the men. "Didn't see ya. Whatcha doin'?"

"What are *you* doing?" Katie bravely yelled back. "I saw you at our house in Oregon last night. Are you following us?"

"That was your house? Oh, er, sorry, no, we were lookin' for somethin' some lady hired us for," the man known as Boris said.

"Wow, they seem okay," Aidan said quietly to his siblings, relieved.

"Yes, so far so good," Katie whispered back.

Katie asked the men, "How did you get here so fast, and what are you looking for?"

"Some lady hired us to find a small bronze box that she thinks is buried under Stonehenge. She paid for us to get over here fast, had a crew dig a big hole in the ground near here, and will pay us a bundle if we can find it and give it to her. First she said it might be near your house in Oregon, but now she thinks it's here. Hey, are you looking for it, too?"

"No. What does she want with it?" asked Katie.

"No clue. Must be important though," Boris said.

"I guess so," replied Katie.

Morgan started sniffing the air and squeaked something to Jeremy, who started running back to the door.

"Hurry up, Katie, let's go! Jeremy and Morgan are running back to the door," Aidan said. "It must be time to go." Scrambling up the path and stairs next to the slide, they could hear their parents' muffled voices.

"Hey, what about those four men back there?" added Aidan.

"Sounds like they have their own way out," Katie said. "Let's go find Mom and Dad!"

Back in the corridor, they heard their parents' voices nearing the other door.

"Mom, Dad, where are you?" Aidan called out.

"Right here," their mother answered, as they reached the corridor, panting a little. Caragh was with them.

Morgan started dancing a jig, and Mom told the family they'd better get a move on up the stairs and back above ground to Stonehenge, where Kubla was still parked.

"Keep the map close!" Caragh called after them. "There are many other families who will want it if they find out about it."

"We will!" Mom replied, as she ushered her family up the stairs pronto. The ground began to rumble again. Toward the top, they were met by a loud, smelly, menacing-looking troll, almost twice the size of Dad.

"What the heck?" bellowed Brian. "Out of our way!"

Morgan chattered something to the troll that was lost on everyone there except the troll, who seemed to understand, quieted down, and moved out of the way.

On their way past him, Jeremy said to the troll, clear as day, "You could use a mint."

Chapter Seven

Back to Manzanita

Back into the fresh air above ground and standing on the soft grass, they felt grateful, relieved, and as peaceful as the large stones.

"Are you all ready to leave?" asked their mom.

From the short distance from where they were standing, they could smell several other pungent grunting trolls climbing up the stairs, hot on their trail.

"Oh no, not again!" said Aidan.

"What do we have to do to get rid of them, and what the heck do they want from us, anyway?!" asked Katie.

She started to turn to talk to them. Knowing that would do no good, Morgan intercepted, putting himself between the Andersons and the trolls. Caragh flew up the stairs and past the angry trolls. Hovering near Morgan and above them all, she moved her right arm horizontally in a half circle above the trolls, suspending them in mid-stomp.

Turning to the Anderson family, she instructed them, "I can't hold them here indefinitely. You have to get back to Kubla and get out of here *now*."

"You don't have to tell us twice. Thank you, Caragh!" Dad yelled back as they high-tailed it to Kubla, still parked nearby.

"Remember to stand sure!" Caragh shouted back after them, as she and the trolls returned below Stonehenge. The ground rumbled again before closing back up.

They scrambled back to their beloved motorhome, with Mom and Dad back at the helm. Morgan, Jeremy, and Aidan started doing the hokey pokey in the middle aisle, and Kubla started up.

"Join us, Katie!" said Aidan.

"Sister, sister, sister!" added Jeremy, as Morgan squeaked joyfully.

"Just a minute," Katie said, curious about what Caragh had just said. After checking with her parents and doing a quick internet search, she made a note in her tablet:

"Stand Sure" is the motto of Clan Anderson. It is
written as a reminder at the bottom of the Anderson
coat of arms, which is a symbol, like a logo, which
represents a family or group of close-knit and

interrelated families (especially associated with families in the Scottish Highlands). During medieval times in Europe, coats of arms were added to outer garments, like cloth tunics, and worn over armor in battle, to shield it from the sun's rays and to identify clans during and after battles. There were many battles between the Scottish and English from 1296-1346, sometimes referred to as the Wars of Scottish Independence. Scottish clans also fought each other for reputation, wealth, territory, and survival. Coats of arms evolved to denote family descent, property ownership, adoption, alliance, and eventually profession. Mottos from Clans in Scotland and England helped each family or tribe feel strong, as there were so many wars between groups for land and resources.

Thinking about how it relates to now, Katie added:

I guess they fought so much and had to keep themselves strong and "Stand Sure" in order to be able to continue fighting, to survive. It's too bad that being peaceful wasn't an option back then. I'm glad things are better now in that way at least. But now there's autism and other problems. There have been many technological advancements, but the world has also become more toxic, so now some babies and

toddlers are being made sick as a result. Back during
medieval times, this kind of stuff didn't happen.
*I sure wish there was a cure for autism **now**. It's so*
hard to be patient. I want my brother back. Just like
in those medieval European battles in which loved
ones' lives were taken, my brother's normal life has
been taken. It's too much loss, but in this case the
person is still alive.

Half way home by now, after Mom and Dad shared what happened, they were all excited to find that precious amulet.

"Our sweet boy," Mom said, sitting next to her husband up front, where their kids couldn't hear them.

"Yes," their dad answered, "thank goodness Aidan and Katie are well."

"Yes, I'm grateful for that. Hey, remember what my mother told us when we first started having kids? It really stuck with me, and I think of it often: 'They'll challenge you like you wouldn't believe, and they might even turn out to be smarter than you are.'"

"Amen to that," their dad answered.

They rode the air all the way back home to Manzanita, where Kubla parked comfortably in its usual spot in front of their house.

Upon landing, Morgan took off his cap and bowed deeply again, finishing his landing dance with Jeremy, Aidan, and Katie with a flourish.

"Group hug! We can do this!" Mom cheered.

Then they walked around the front yard to the garden shed in the back to get their shovels, hopes high.

"Let's get to work!" Dad said.

Chapter Eight

The Front Yard

"Where's the treasure map?" Mom asked Dad after they'd all reassembled.

"Right here in my front pocket," answered Dad, patting his pocket. He took it out, and opened it up to share with everyone. I'm glad we still have some daylight."

After getting their shovels and reassembling in the front yard, Katie studied the map and said, "looks like it's in the middle near our house and close to where Kubla parked. The legend on the map says it's buried between one and two feet deep. Morgan, do you know how to use a shovel to dig?"

"Morgan dig too, Morgan dig too!" sang Jeremy.

Morgan smiled and spun his tail in a circle. This time sparkly dust swirled around, and they watched as he magically dug a two-foot deep, five-foot long trench.

"Wow, you're a handy guy to have around!" Mom said to Morgan, impressed. "This will take no time at all." Morgan squeaked and Jeremy smiled.

While they dug, or rather mostly watched Morgan dig, a car pulled up in front of their house and parked there. No one got out.

"I wonder who that is," said Katie.

"Geez, not again," Aidan groaned.

"Lions and tigers and bears, oh my!" said Jeremy.

"Let's go talk with them, Fiona," said their dad to their mom. "Keep up the good work here—Morgan, kids!"

As soon as Mom and Dad started walking towards the car, it sped off.

"That was weird," said Mom.

"Sure was," her husband agreed, shrugging. "How's it going, kids?" he called as they walked back.

"Great. I think we've struck something," said Aidan, having just heard a bonk on something hard below ground.

Morgan swirled his tail specifically around whatever the object was, and this time the sparkly dust formed a half circle before descending into the ground below, like a rounded shovel.

"What is it?" Katie asked.

They watched amazed, as Morgan's sparkly dust hardened into a strong fishing-net-like object while underground, and pulled up some rocks and fossils.

"That's cool. But not it," Aidan said.

"Dang," added Katie.

Dad made a decision. "How about we take a break from all this for now and go cut down one of the smallish Douglas fir trees in our backyard for our Christmas tree?"

Great idea, Brian." Mom said to her husband, as they all headed toward the backyard. "What with all this going on, I almost forgot that Christmas is only a few days away!"

Once back in the house, with their Christmas tree up and decorated, the family settled down after dinner. Dad, Mom, and Aidan were playing Monopoly—their favorite board game—while Jeremy sat looking at the tree, talking to himself the whole time, mostly quoting lines from movies he'd seen over and over.

Katie started another internet search.

"Mom and Dad, it would've been fun to see the solstice while we were at Stonehenge," Katie said. "Check out this beautiful photo of a winter solstice sunrise through two of the large stones, that I found online."

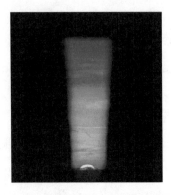

"Wow! That's something!" agreed Dad. "How about if we go back next year, just for fun? We're on a mission now—for Jeremy."

"Yes!" Mom and Katie answered in unison.

Bright and early the next morning, the family returned to their front yard.

They'd had a floodlight on it all night, plus when they went in for dinner the evening before, they called the police about a possible intruder after seeing that parked car take off.

Because those four men at Stonehenge had trespassed in their front yard earlier, it all added up to something suspicious. They were almost used to strange things happening by now, like trolls chasing them, because of Morgan's magical help and occasional predicaments over the years, but they just didn't know what to expect.

"Let's get back to digging," Mom reminded them all.

Morgan sprang into action.

"There's only about 200 square feet left to check out. We can do it!" Dad said, pointing to the map. "With Morgan's help, that is. We sure appreciate you," he said to Morgan. Morgan bowed and smiled.

Wanting to help find the amulet faster too, Katie sat down in front of their house, near Kubla, and closed her eyes. Full of questions, she began swaying from side to side again, focusing on some of the *wh* questions they were trying to teach Jeremy, like *who, what, where,* and *why,* as they relate to the brass box. The other Katie appeared to her again, in front of her, but invisible to everyone else.

"What's up with Katie?" asked Dad.

"She did this when we were underground at Stonehenge, too," Aidan told them, less concerned this time since she had pulled out of it then. "I think she'll be okay. It seems to be something she needs to do sometimes."

Morgan stopped searching and looked at Katie, knowing it wouldn't be long now. Morgan squeaked something to Jeremy.

"Soon!" exclaimed Jeremy, smiling at his brother. He and Morgan started dancing near Katie, and now sparkly rainbow dust was falling around the whole family.

Katie stopped swaying.

Chapter Nine

The Amulet

"Hi Katie," her translucent self opposite her said, "the bronze box with its precious contents is a treasure in more ways than one. For people who need the amulet, it can appear once in their lifetime—if they are lucky, that is."

"Do you know why? And for that matter, how?" Katie asked.

"No I don't. It could be only God does. I'm sure glad Jeremy seems to have been chosen, though. His heart is pure. The amulet has the power to heal Jeremy completely. He will have a good and normal life. You won't have to worry about him any longer. Your whole family can finally go back to normal."

"Good, that's a relief," Katie said. "How about those people who parked in front of our house, and then took off when Mom and Dad went to talk with them? And those four men who were here before our trip, and then at Stonehenge when we were there. Are they after the same thing?"

"Yes they are, but don't be afraid of them. They may seem like a threat, but they aren't," Katie's other self answered. "Remember, you are like Joan of Arc, the bravest of the brave: 'No fear, only love.'"

"Thank you. I always appreciate talking with you," Katie said.

"You're most welcome. Remember, stand sure," her translucent self called, as she faded away.

Katie came to again, her family standing close by, keeping an eye on her. She felt resolute.

"Let's try digging right here," she told them, standing up and pointing to the exact spot where she had been sitting.

Morgan grinned and did a somersault, gleeful. Relieved and grateful to see Katie okay, Aidan and their parents gave her a hug while Morgan danced.

Jeremy said, "sister okay" again but didn't want a hug. He had loved hugs as a baby, then autism took hold when he was 19 months old.

Katie, as she often did, said a prayer, hoping his recovery was close.

"Morgan, do you want to do the honors?" Katie asked. Morgan bowed to them all, then waved, sprinkling more sparkly dust into the air, which landed exactly on that spot.

Just then, a car pulled up in front of their house, parked, and this time turned the engine off.

"You've got to be kidding me," Katie said, as the rest of the family agreed with groans.

It was the same car as before. Mom and Dad exchanged looks.

"Let's go," said Mom. "Wait here."

"Do you want to do the honors?" Mom asked Dad.

"Sure," he said, as they walked over to the parked car. The two people in the car got out. The family recognized them immediately.

Surprised, Mom asked their family friend, Loreta, "Hey, what's going on here, you guys? Was that you last time? I didn't recognize your car. We're right in the middle of something important here."

Loreta and her young son Harry, Jeremy's age, stood near them. Harry was hopping around and making sounds similar to Jeremy's, while Loreta started to explain.

"Yes, that was us, and it's a new car. You know how much we're trying to heal Harry, just like you all are trying to heal Jeremy, right?"

"Yes, of course," answered Fiona.

From behind them, close to the house, Jeremy, was excited to see his school buddy. He jumped up and down, yelling, "Chocolate ice cream, chocolate ice cream now! Harry, Harry, Harry! Chocolate ice cream now!"

Harry repeated, "chocolate ice cream now, chocolate ice cream now!"

"We'll be right back, if that's okay with you?" Loreta said, "now *does* seem like a good time for chocolate ice cream."

"Okay, take your time," said Dad. Much to everyone's relief, Loreta and Harry left for the store. They're family friends, but right now this was too much.

"Loreta must have her reasons," said Mom, "but this is definitely unexpected."

Mom and Dad returned to the spot to dig. Once again, Morgan bowed to them all and sprinkled more sparkly dust into the air. A net formed again, scooping up a large half-circle of dirt. The magic net shook so that the dirt fell through it, leaving bigger chunks of earth along with a gold-colored object.

It was the bronze box! They all held their breath, while Morgan picked it out of the net, cleaned the dirt off quickly until it was shiny, and presented it to Jeremy with flourish.

Jeremy looked at it, took it from Morgan, and started hitting his head with it, letting out four short ear-piercing screams.

"Is something hurting, Jeremy?" their mom asked, scared and not knowing what to do, as usual when this happened. She knew the doctors didn't either—she'd tried hard for years. She and Brian felt powerless to help their son recover.

Jeremy didn't answer.

"How about taking some deep breaths? That will help," she added, hopefully.

Katie and Aidan watched him, both feeling near tears.

Morgan jumped on Jeremy's shoulder and Jeremy calmed down. They all breathed a sigh of relief.

"Thank goodness," their mom answered. Their dad gave Jeremy a little hug, though it seemed like Jeremy didn't really want one, as usual, lately.

"It's okay, honey, go ahead and open it," said their mom, nodding at the small bronze box Jeremy still held in his hand.

Jeremy turned the lever on the latch, and the lid sprang open. Inside was a dark-green-colored velvet pouch. He lifted it out carefully and pulled the pouch drawstrings. A gentle, glowing light emanated from it. He poured the golden bejeweled amulet from the bag into his hand, smiling, and closed his eyes. Glittering rubies, diamonds, and emeralds shone up at him from all around the small glowing object, lighting up his face. He closed his hand around the amulet. He was instantly calmed and his facial expression changed.

Chapter Ten

Secrets Revealed

In fact, Jeremy's whole demeanor and stance changed, and he looked more like Aidan and Katie with every passing second.

"How are you feeling, Jeremy"? their mom asked him.

Jeremy was quiet and looked all around, at his family and at Morgan. He looked at their house and at Kubla, then down at the glowing amulet he was holding. He seemed a little dazed, but also very relieved.

Morgan squeaked excitedly. Jeremy looked at him for a few seconds. Morgan squeaked again, watching Jeremy, who smiled and nodded to Morgan. They're connection remained strong.

Suddenly, Caragh appeared.

"Caragh?" Mom and Dad said together.

"It is done," Caragh said solemnly.

Looking around at each of them, Jeremy said, "Hi, Mom, Dad, Katie, Aidan, Morgan. Who are you?" he asked, looking at Caragh.

"My dear boy, I'm your Fairie Godmother. Your family loves you very much, so they went to Stonehenge looking for something to help you feel better. Your parents found me, and I gave them a map to find this amulet.

"The amulet you're holding cured you of autism. You are free now. Your brain is restored, along with your gut and its normal flora. The gastrointestinal discomfort, confusion, brain inflammation, headaches, self-injurious behavior, and anxiety are all gone now. No more hurtful and disrespectful behavior from other people now that you have fully recovered. You can communicate with others easily now, and have a good life, and when you grow up, you can of course be independent—marry and have children if you want to, have meaningful, respectable work that you enjoy, buy your own home, car, groceries, and everything else you need for yourself. Everything will be normal for you from now on—plus you can travel if you choose to, and live on your own terms. You are safe. Life is your oyster now, and you can live with ease. Your family can, too."

"Wow," said Jeremy. "Thank you!" The new way of being and feeling was sinking in.

Katie cried happy tears. They all did. She hugged her little brother. Very, very appreciative, the whole family gave Jeremy a group hug. And this time, he hugged them back.

Overwhelmed, there were no words. It had been going on for so long. The pain was over now. It was a dream come true.

They stammered their way through many questions, and Caragh addressed them all, reassuring them.

Katie remembered and recorded in her tablet, for future reference, a Winston Churchill quote she remembered their mom saying a few years ago:

"Never give up on something you can't go a day without thinking about."

Loreta and Harry drove up again and parked in front. After getting out of their car, Harry yelled loudly, jumping all around and flapping his hands excitedly. "Chocolate ice cream!"

"I know him, right?" Jeremy asked his parents.

"Yes, Jeremy, that's your best friend, Harry," answered Mom.

"Oh, right. I remember," Jeremy said. "Well, I love chocolate ice cream. We all do, right?"

"Yes, dear. I'm glad you remember," their dad answered.

"Do you want to talk with them now, or maybe wait until later?" Mom asked Jeremy.

"Now is okay, but just for a little while," said Jeremy. "I'm tired."

"Tell us when you need quiet time, okay?" said their Mom. "A nap is probably a good idea for you today."

"Thanks, Mom. I feel much better," said Jeremy.

"Hi, Harry," Jeremy greeted his friend, as he and his mom walked toward them.

Right away, Harry and Loreta noticed the change in Jeremy, as well as the still-glowing amulet he was holding.

Harry didn't answer this time and jumped up and down excitedly. Language was extra hard for him. Autism varies from person to person.

Morgan squeaked some news. Then he bowed to the two boys. He knew all that Jeremy had endured, and all that Harry still endured in this life. Both boys understood Morgan perfectly.

Loreta looked at their mom, having pieced together what had just happened, and went to give her a hug.

"Wait a minute, Loreta," Mom said, stopping her. "Did you send those four men to our home to search for this magical amulet? And then to Stonehenge after it?"

"Yes, that was me," confessed Loreta. "I'm sorry. You know how hard this is. I meant no offense, just trying so hard to get him well."

"I understand, Loreta," said Mom. "But there was no need to scare us, trick us, or take from us. The amulet was on our land, apparently intended for us. How did you find out about it, anyway? We didn't even know until Caragh told us."

"Well, have you ever noticed how sometimes I know things before they're announced at school? I don't know how, but sometimes I get feelings and ideas that turn out to be real. I've learned to trust them over the years," replied Loreta, "so when I started seeing you all in my mind's eye with an amulet that holds the power to heal, I thought, 'maybe Harry can finally be well and have a normal life'.

"I'm desperate for him to recover. I know it wasn't okay, and again, I'm sorry," said Loreta.

"As gifted as you are, Loreta, it would have been best if you'd been able to put your desperation aside, and just talked with Brian and me instead of doing all this scary, wild stuff. We might have been able to work something out ahead of time," said Mom.

"You're right," Loreta agreed.

"Caragh, what do you think?" Mom asked.

"I see that Loreta was acting from fear and didn't think it through," said Caragh. "The forgiveness, friendship, and trust are up to you. Jeremy and your family are my focus this time, but I might be able to help with healing another child in addition—if there are special circumstances, as I told you and Brian back at Stonehenge. Jeremy's recovery is locked in."

She turned to Jeremy with compassion. "If you want to share the amulet, Jeremy, I'll do my best to extend its power to Harry."

Jeremy spoke up. "Harry is my best friend. I want him to be well, too."

Harry, very uncharacteristically, hugged Jeremy.

"Here, Harry, hold the amulet," Jeremy enunciated perfectly to his friend, passing the glowing amulet to Harry.

"Morgan, if this is going to work a second time today, I'll need reinforcement from you, please," Caragh said.

Bowing graciously, Morgan eagerly somersaulted over to them and stood next to Caragh.

"Everyone join hands, with Harry in the middle," said Caragh. Then she added, "focus on feeling 'no fear, only love.'"

They all felt it—an overwhelming sense of love surrounding them.

Holding the powerful amulet, Harry looked up and smiled.

"Hey Mom, I'm tired. I could use a nap soon. But I think the ice cream is starting to melt. Jeremy, do you still want some?" Harry spoke completely normally.

"You bet," Jeremy answered, and hugged his bestie.

Your Notes

Just like Katie writes notes to remember things and refer back to later, please feel free to write notes about things you are learning or want to learn more about, your thoughts and feelings, hopes and dreams, and things that make you happy, here:

Author's Note

For parents, librarians, other adults, or teen readers:

Autism, PANDAS/PANS, Lyme, Bartonella, and other diseases, infections, and disorders can change babies, children, and adults so much that they are not whom they would have been otherwise. This is an understatement especially when such conditions are triggered due to toxins, etc., from the environment that affect babies for the rest of their lives. If mild enough or with the right interventions early on, some recover. I know four who have. For those who don't recover—even when the family is doing everything known to help their loved one reach their full potential and live as happy and healthy a life as possible—parents often wish they could outlive their adult child.

In Marcia Hinds's book, *I Know You're in There: Winning Our War Against Autism*, her recovered adult son, Ryan Hinds, says, "Some people think we should just accept autism. And that if a child is treated, it changes who that kid is. I am still the same person I was, only now I'm happy and can enjoy life. It is hard to understand that children are not receiving proper medical treatment because some people think we should celebrate autism. When doctors believe the medical issues associated with autism are just part of a 'developmental disorder,' children are not treated for the same medical conditions as every other kid. Is that really okay?"

This story is my effort to entertain and educate all readers, children and adults alike, in hopes of making the world a better place for everyone through understanding, one reader at a time, and to also send the message that we still need cures and more safe and effective medical treatments for autism that work for everyone, not only a few.

I am grateful for those who support neurodiversity, whatever the cause, and pray the world becomes a better place when it comes to accepting and appreciating neurodiverse individuals, as well as others who experience other ways of being in life.

Everyone is equal and deserving of the same respect. Gender, race, and ability or disability have no effect on one's worth as a human being.

I hope you enjoy and learn good things from this story.

Acknowledgements

Many thanks to Yvonne Aileen, Sara Pehrsson, Ali Shaw, and Janis Hunt Johnson. Your excellent advice and support during the writing, editing, and publishing process have been so important to me.

About the Author

Cate Read Hickman was born and raised in the San Francisco Bay Area, and has lived in Oregon for the past few decades. This is the first book in the *Morgan the Motorhome Mouse and the Andersons* series. Join Morgan soon for more family adventures.

Made in the USA
Thornton, CO
09/09/23 06:11:57

d280e862-6d84-4de7-8090-ace9c767889bR01